Presented to

Spring Branch Memorial Library

By

**Area Residents Through the
Friends of the Library Buy-A-Book
Campaign**

Henry and Mudge
and the
Tall Tree House

The Twenty-First Book of Their Adventures

Story by Cynthia Rylant
Pictures by Carolyn Bracken
in the style of Suçie Stevenson

SIMON & SCHUSTER BOOKS FOR YOUNG READERS
New York   London   Toronto   Sydney   Singapore

To Joe and Dean, good uncles—CR

THE HENRY AND MUDGE BOOKS

SIMON & SCHUSTER BOOKS FOR YOUNG READERS
An imprint of Simon & Schuster Children's Publishing Division
1230 Avenue of the Americas
New York, New York 10020
Text copyright © 2002 by Cynthia Rylant
Illustrations copyright © 2002 by Suçie Stevenson
SIMON & SCHUSTER BOOKS FOR YOUNG READERS is a trademark of Simon & Schuster.

Book design by Mark Siegel
The text of this book is set in 18-point Goudy.
The illustrations are rendered in pen-and-ink and watercolor.
Manufactured in the United States of America

10   9   8   7   6   5   4

Library of Congress Cataloging-in-Publication Data
Rylant, Cynthia. Henry and Mudge and the tall tree house: the twenty-first book of their adventures /
story by Cynthia Rylant; pictures by Suçie Stevenson.
p. cm.—(The Henry and Mudge books)
Summary: Henry is excited when his uncle Jake builds him a tree house but worries that his dog Mudge will
not be able to enjoy it with him.
ISBN 978-0-689-81173-9   0313 LAK
[1. Tree houses—Fiction. 2. Dogs—Fiction. 3. Uncles—Fiction.]
I. Stevenson, Suçie, ill. II. Title III. Series: Rylant, Cynthia. Henry and Mudge books.
PZ7-R982Heas   1999
[Fic]—dc21
98-20938
CIP
AC

Contents

Uncle Jake

One day Uncle Jake
came to visit Henry
and Henry's big dog, Mudge,
and Henry's parents.

Uncle Jake was very big.

Henry's father called him "burly."

"What does 'burly' mean?"

Henry asked his father.

"Big, hairy, and plaid,"

said Henry's father.

That was Uncle Jake.

Henry liked Uncle Jake a lot.
Mudge liked him even more.
Mudge liked Uncle Jake
because Uncle Jake *wrestled*.

Mudge and Uncle Jake
would get on the floor
and wrestle and wrestle.

8

Mudge always won.

This time when Uncle Jake
came to visit,
he had something special
in his truck.
He had boards.
"What are the boards for,
Uncle Jake?" asked Henry.

Uncle Jake gave a burly smile
and said, "Adventure."

"Really?" said Henry.

He liked adventure.

Especially with Mudge.

"Yep, I'm building you a *tree house*,"

said Uncle Jake.

"A tree house?" said Henry.

"Wow!"

Henry loved tree houses.

They were thrilling.

They were exciting.

They were . . . *in trees.*   13

Henry looked at Mudge.

Mudge could jump.
Mudge could run.
Mudge could even
dance a little.

14

But Mudge, for sure, could not
climb a tree.
"Uh-oh," thought Henry.
He put his arm around Mudge
and began to worry.

Uncle Jake was very proud.

Henry was very worried.

Mudge was just itchy.

"Okay, Henry, it's all yours,"

said Uncle Jake.

"Go on up!"

Henry looked at Mudge.
Henry did not want
to go into the tree house.
He did not want adventure
without Mudge.
But he couldn't hurt
Uncle Jake's feelings.
He climbed up.   19

He stood in the tree house
and looked around.
It was thrilling.
It was exciting.
It was lonely.
"Thanks, Uncle Jake,"
Henry called.
"It's great."

21

"I'll take Mudge
for a walk,"
said Uncle Jake.
"Have a ball!"
Henry watched Mudge
leave with Uncle Jake.

22

Mudge didn't want to go.
Henry could tell because
Mudge kept sitting down
and yawning.
Mudge always acted tired
when he didn't want to go.
"Sleepy dog!" Uncle Jake
called with a smile.

24

Finally he got Mudge
down the road.
And Henry felt sadder
than any boy with a
new tree house ever felt.

Forgot Something

Henry sat in his tree house

for fourteen minutes.

Then he climbed down

and went into the house.

Uncle Jake was back.

He and Henry's parents

were playing cards. 29

"I forgot something!"
Henry told them.
He ran upstairs.
Mudge was on Henry's bed,
chewing a bone.
Henry gave Mudge
a big hug and kiss
and ran back downstairs.

He waved to his parents
and Uncle Jake, then
returned to the tree house.

He sat
for fourteen minutes.

Then he climbed down and went
into the house.

"Forgot something else!"
he called.

He ran upstairs.

He came back down.

He returned to the tree house
for fourteen more minutes.

Then he climbed back down and went into the house.

"Forgot something!"

He did the same thing over and over.

Five times in a row.

Finally Henry's father
met him at the door.
"Henry, what is it?"
asked Henry's father.
Henry hung his head.
"I miss Mudge."
Henry's father smiled.
"I thought you might,"
he said.
"So Uncle Jake and I
came up with a plan."

35

Very Happy

"Isn't this great, Mudge?"
asked Henry.
They were sitting in
the tree house.
They had comic books
and cheese sandwiches.
Mudge had some toys:
a bear, an alligator,
and a roly-poly snowman.
They were very happy.
A tree house in a tree was okay.

But a tree house in Henry's room
was even better!
It was thrilling.
It was exciting.

It had Mudge.